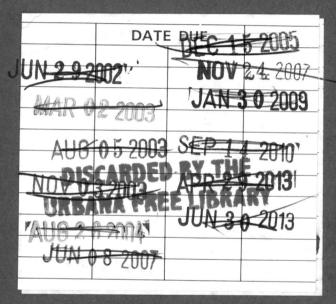

Robin Hood and His Merry Men

Other books by Jane Louise Curry

ROBIN HOOD
and His Merry Men

retold by
JANE LOUISE CURRY
illustrated by
JOHN LYTLE

Margaret K. McElderry Books

For Remson
—J.L.C.

Margaret K. McElderry Books
An imprint of Simon & Schuster Children's Publishing Division
1230 Avenue of the Americas
New York, New York 10020
Text copyright © 1994 by Jane Louise Curry
Illustrations copyright © 1994 by John Lytle
Designed by Nancy Williams
The text of this book is set in Bembo.
The illustrations are rendered in pencil and ink.
Printed in the United States of America.
10 9 8 7 6 5 4 3 2 1
Library of Congress Cataloging-in-Publication Data
Curry, Jane Louise.
Robin Hood and his Merry Men / Jane Louise Curry ; illustrated by John Lytle.
— 1st ed.
p.   cm.
Summary: Recounts the life and adventures of Robin Hood, who, with his band
of followers, lived in Sherwood Forest as an outlaw dedicated to fighting tyranny.
ISBN 0-689-50609-0
1. Robin Hood (Legendary character)—Legends.   [1. Robin Hood (Legendary
character)   2. Folklore—England.]   I. Robin Hood (Legend). English.
II. Lytle, John, ill.   III. Title.
PZ8.1.C97Ro   1994
398.22—dc20   94-14023

Retold from the fifteenth-century poem "A Lytell Geste of Robyn Hode."

Contents

How Robin Became an Outlaw

On the Christmas when Robin Hood was fifteen years old, he left Barnesdale and went to stay until summer with his uncle, Sir George Gamwell, at Gamwell Hall.

Robin's uncle had no children, and he loved Robin like a son. For Christmas he gave him many gifts. He gave him a new bow and a quiver full of arrows. He gave him a suit of Lincoln-green cloth, a handsome horse, and a fine saddle too.

"Now I am ready for adventure!" said Robin.

Nothing exciting ever happened at Gamwell Hall, but in April the king came north to Nottingham.

"May I ride to Nottingham Town tomorrow?" Robin asked. "There is to be a shooting contest. The king will be there to give the prize."

"Yes, you may go," said Sir George. "But do not ride through Sherwood Forest. The robbers who live there will steal your fine horse."

On the day of the archery contest, Robin rose early.

He dressed in his best. Then he saddled his horse and rode off at a trot.

Before long he came to six foresters walking toward the town. Like Robin each had a bow and a quiver of arrows slung across his back. They wore the king's badge on their hats. Sherwood and the other great forests in England belonged to the king. All of the deer and other beasts in the forests belonged to him, too.

"Good morning," Robin called. "Are you going to the shooting match?"

"We are," they answered.

The shortest forester waved his bow. "And Peter of Pitchley will win the prize!"

"Oh, no!" said Robin. "For I, Robin of Barnesdale, will be shooting, too."

The foresters laughed.

"Now, there's a fine joke!" said the tallest. "Beardless babies do not shoot before the king."

"Pooh!" said another. "You cannot even bend that long bow you carry."

Robin began to be angry. He stopped his horse and leaped to the ground. "Can a baby hit the young beech tree by the bend in the road ahead?" He pointed. "I have twenty silver shillings that say I can."

The foresters laughed even louder than before.

"Foolish boy!" one cried.

"You cannot shoot half so far," called another.

"You might as well try for yonder deer, the hart that

stands at the edge of the forest," said a third.

Robin's cheeks grew red with anger.

"No, brothers." The tallest forester raised his hand. "The babe has made his bet. Let him aim and shoot as he wishes."

Robin fitted an arrow to his bowstring. "Then I choose the hart that stands at the edge of the forest," he said.

"Impossible!" cried the foresters, for the deer stood far beyond the beech tree.

Robin Hood bent his bow, took aim, and let fly.

The arrow flew, straight and true, past the beech tree and on. The stag gave a leap, then a stagger, and fell.

The foresters stared. Robin laughed.

"There is meat for your dinners," he said. "And twenty shillings for me!"

"Twenty shillings?" the tallest forester roared. "Not a penny, proud boy! You have killed the king's deer. You will pay a fat price for that! Take him, men! Tie him tight."

With a shout the six foresters rushed at Robin. But Robin was younger and faster than they. He ran for his horse and leaped to his saddle. His horse ran away like the wind.

"Stop!" called the foresters. "In the king's name, stop!" They raised their bows and sent a flock of arrows flying after Robin.

Not one touched him, but the last arrow hit his

beautiful horse on its hip. The horse stumbled, then raced on. Robin turned in his saddle, aimed his bow, and sent back a sharp answer.

The unlucky arrow flew all too straight. It struck the tall forester, and he dropped to the ground.

Robin's anger turned to alarm. He had shot without thinking. What if the man were dead? Even if he were not, the deer was. Men went to prison for killing the king's deer.

In his fright Robin rode straight into Sherwood Forest. He could not go home. He could never go home. The foresters knew he was Robin of Barnesdale, and soon the king would, too. The king would declare him an outlaw. The sheriff of Nottingham would ride out to arrest him!

But Robin was young, and brave. He saw the sunlight and the broad oak trees of Sherwood Forest and the bluebells in their shade. If he could not go home, then why not—

Why not stay in Sherwood? His uncle said robbers and poachers lived in the forest. Well, then! He would join them and live a merry life in the greenwood.

And so he rode on.

ROBIN HOOD AND LITTLE JOHN

In Sherwood Forest Robin Hood found more brave
fellows than bad ones, though almost all of them were
outlaws. Some were poachers, poor men who hunted
the king's deer to feed their families. Some were robbers. Some were farmers who had lost their farms to
the greedy sheriff and his tax collectors. They had
brought their families to live in the forest. Some of
the men were only boys. They had come because
their parents had too many mouths to feed at home.

Robin soon became the best hunter in Sherwood.
He was the fastest climber of trees, the speediest run-
ner, and the merriest maker of mischief. When he
grew older, the outlaws made him their leader.

The outlaws led a merry life. They held wrestling
matches and shooting contests. Every day they hunted the king's deer. They shared their food with poor
travelers. Rich travelers had to pay for their dinners—
often with all the money they had in their purses.

Afterward Robin and his men gave almost every penny to the poor.

On some days, though, nothing happened at all. On one such day Robin grew bored with eating and singing and telling tall tales.

"I shall walk out into the wide world to seek an adventure," he told his men.

"We will go with you!" they said.

"No," said Robin. "Stay. If I need you I will sound my horn."

Near the edge of the forest Robin came to a brook that ran merrily among the trees. A log lay across it. On the far side Robin saw a stranger hurrying toward the log bridge.

"Stop, fellow!" Robin called. "These are my woods and this is my bridge. *I* will cross first."

"Indeed!" the stranger roared. "No one commands John Little. *I* shall cross first."

The stranger's voice was as deep as he was tall. His staff was as stout as a young tree. He set his foot firmly on the log.

Robin planted a foot on his end of the log. "Hold where you are, Longlegs!" he warned. He reached for an arrow to fit to his bow.

The stranger laughed. He strode three steps nearer.

"One more inch and I will put an arrow through your foot," said Robin.

"For shame!" the tall stranger boomed. "A longbow

against a poor man's staff? That is a coward's threat."

Robin grew red in the face. He threw down his bow. "No one shall call me coward! Stand where you are. I will cut a staff of my own."

Robin found a thicket of young oak trees. There he cut himself a good, strong staff. Then he hurried back to the bridge and the bold stranger.

"Now I'll thump you like a drum, Longlegs!" said Robin. "He who knocks the other into the water will win. Agreed?"

"Agreed." The tall stranger moved toward Robin. He lifted his staff.

Robin laughed and bounded at him. He ducked low and gave the stranger a blow on the hip. The stranger staggered.

"Oho!" the stranger cried. "That's a gift I shall repay!" In a flash he gave Robin a crack on the crown.

The fight grew fierce. Robin and the stranger knocked and jabbed. They whacked and whanged. They thumped and thwacked.

Robin was used to winning at every game he played. Yet now, for every blow Robin landed, the stranger gave one back. At last Robin lost his temper. He took a wild swing at the stranger's head, and to his surprise felt a hard blow to his own middle. He fell into the brook with a splash.

The stranger peered all around. "Ho, my fine rooster!" he jeered. "Where are you? I do not see you on your bridge."

Robin Hood sat, up to his neck in the stream. He laughed in spite of himself. "I am in my brook," he said.

As he stood up he raised his horn and blew a loud note. The sound rang through the forest. Men in green came racing through the trees. They came in twos and threes. Soon there were forty and more.

Will Stutely, a yeoman from Barnesdale, like Robin, came first. "What's this?" he asked. "Here's Robin, wet to the skin!"

Robin grinned. "I always tumble into trouble when I lose my temper. This fellow knocked me into the brook."

The outlaws took hold of the stranger. "Then he shall have a ducking, too," they cried.

"Hold!" Robin raised a hand to stop them. "He is a good fighter and a cheerful fellow. He beat me fairly."

To the stranger he said, "Join us. We will give you a fine yew bow and a merry life."

"And every year a good suit of Lincoln green," added Much, the miller's son.

The stranger laughed. "Then John Little is your man. But who are you?"

"My name is Robin Hood. He who holds your elbow is Will Stutely. The fellow in the scarlet hood is Will Scadlock."

"We call him Will Scarlet," said Much. "And you, John Little, we should call Little John."

At that the outlaws all laughed, for Little John was nearly seven feet tall.

"A fine name," Robin agreed. "Come, then, Little John! Tonight we shall feast and make merry."

And that is what they did.

LITTLE JOHN AND THE SHERIFF

One Wednesday when Little John had nothing else to do, he took his new bow to Nottingham. On that day every week archers came to practice target shooting. People from the town went to the castle field to watch them.

"Good welcome to you, stranger," the watchers said to Little John. "Yours is a long longbow indeed! Come, show us how well you can shoot."

Little John stepped up to the line and fitted an arrow to his bowstring. He raised the bow, gave a mighty pull, and shot.

Thwang-g-g! The arrow drove deep into the center of the target.

The watchers stared. "Did you see? He did not even stop to aim."

Four times Little John took a turn at a target. Four times men moved it farther down the field. Four times Little John's arrow flew straight to the bull's-eye.

"Hurrah for the stranger!" all the townspeople cheered.

One fat watcher wore a fine blue cloak with a fox fur collar. On his hat he wore a bright gold badge. His nose was sharp and his eyes were cold. "What is your name, Longlegs?" he asked.

"My name is—Reynold Greenleaf," Little John answered.

"I am the sheriff of Nottingham," the sharp-nosed man said with a sniff. "I can use a master archer like yourself. I will pay you twenty gold marks a year."

Oho! thought Little John to himself. The wicked sheriff! Now, here's a good chance for mischief. So he grinned as if he were a simpleton who had never been to town before. "Yes, please, Sir Sheriff, sir." And he followed the sheriff home to his house.

The next night the sheriff said, "Tomorrow I ride out for three days' hunting. I have the king's leave to hunt his deer. I shall stay at Kirkby. You will be my watchman here at home."

"Yes, Sir Sheriff." Little John nodded. "Not even a fly shall pass by me."

The next morning Little John stood guard at the door as his new master and two of his huntsmen rode away. Then he went back to bed. When he grew weary of sleeping, he began to be hungry.

"Ho, steward!" he called. "Bring me meat and drink!"

"I will not," came the answer. "Lazy dogs get no meat."

Little John grumbled and went to find the butler.

"Cut me a dish of bread and meat," he said.

"No work, no pork," the butler growled. He shut his door with a bang.

So Little John went to the kitchen and banged on the table.

"Cook! Bread and beef and a bottle to drink!"

"You are not master here," the cook roared. He lifted a fist as huge as a ham and hard as a hammer. With it he gave Little John a good knock.

"Oho!" said Little John. "You are a good fellow, but I always return a rap for a tap."

"You can try." The cook grinned and took hold of a stout rolling pin.

Little John snatched up a long iron ladle and swung it. The cook blocked the blow with his rolling pin. Back and forth they went. The ladle and rolling pin clanged. The cook and Little John bashed and smashed and batted and banged until they were weary. Neither could land a blow on the other.

"By Saint George!" Little John laughed. "Can you shoot as well as you swing a rolling pin?"

"Almost." The cook put down his rolling pin. From the cupboard he brought a loaf of bread and a dish of beef.

Little John cut himself a slice of each. "Then come with me to Robin Hood in Sherwood Forest."

"Why should I?" asked the cook.

"Because the sheriff is a bad master and a worse man," Little John said. "He robs the poor to make himself rich. Robin Hood's men rob the rich and greedy to feed the poor and needy. In Sherwood you will have a new yew bow, a suit of Lincoln green, silver in your purse, and a merry life in the bargain."

The cook waved a beef bone. "Lead, and I will follow! But first, come follow me."

Little John followed the cook to the sheriff's treasure room. The door was shut fast with six stout locks, but they broke them with an iron bar.

"Bless me!" said Little John. "There is silver enough to buy food for all the poor in the county!"

So they filled bags with silver platters, plates and spoons, and silver pitchers and drinking cups. Best of all, in a silver pitcher, they found a sack of silver pennies and a purse full of gold coins.

With four bags full, they hurried to the stable. There they saddled two horses and rode out through the town and away.

"To Sherwood!" shouted Little John.

"To Sherwood!" cried the cook.

THE SHERIFF COMES TO SHERWOOD

When Little John and the sheriff's cook came to the camp in the forest, Little John called out, "Ho, Robin! See what gifts the sheriff sends us! We have a cook and two horses, and silver to eat from. And here are silver pennies and gold for the poor."

But Robin was not pleased. "Surely the sheriff did not send these gifts. You have stolen them."

The cook was surprised. "But, Master, *you* rob the rich to give to the poor."

"We do," said Robin. "But first we give them a good meal and a merry one. We make them pay a pretty penny for it, but we are not sneak thieves."

"Very well," said Little John. "Then I will make it all right." He leaped onto his stolen horse and rode out of Sherwood at a gallop.

Halfway to Kirkby Little John saw the sheriff and his companions, out hunting. "Master, Master!" he called.

The sheriff turned back to meet him. "Reynold Greenleaf! Why are you here?"

"Oh, Master!" cried Little John. "I have seen a great marvel! Not five miles from here. A green hart!"

The sheriff laughed. "Deer are not green, you great booby. You saw green light through the green leaves."

"Oh, no," said Little John. "This hart was green from antler to hoof. A herd of forty followed him."

"Truly?" The sheriff's eyes shone, for he had seen no deer all day. "Then, good Greenleaf, your hart can be green or brown or purple. Lead the way and I will follow."

Little John turned back toward Sherwood Forest. The sheriff came close behind. His two huntsmen followed. At dinnertime they rode into the outlaws' camp.

"See, Master," Little John said to the sheriff. "There is the great green hart." He pointed to Robin Hood in his suit of Lincoln green.

The sheriff grew pale. "Alas, Reynold Greenleaf, you have led me into a den of robbers!"

"It serves you right," said Little John. "At your house I was not fed enough to keep a mouse alive."

Robin Hood laughed. "We will serve you better here, Sir Sheriff. Tonight you shall be one of us. Come share our meal."

The sheriff sat down in gloom. Roast venison and loaves of bread were served on his own silver platters. He ate from one of his own silver plates. The outlaws filled his silver cup with ale from his own silver pitcher. He was so sad to see his treasures in the forest that he could hardly eat.

After dark the outlaws settled down to sleep. Little John pointed to the ground beneath the greenwood trees. "Here is your bed, Master, next to mine."

The ground was hard. The night was long. The sheriff shivered and sighed, and his sides grew sore. By morning he was stiff as a stone.

"Good morrow, Sheriff," Robin Hood greeted him. "How do you like our life here in the greenwood?"

The sheriff groaned. "I could not take another night of it for all the gold in England."

"Nonsense," Robin said. "Give us a year. We will make a fine outlaw of you."

"No, no! Not one night more," the sheriff cried. "Let me go or shoot me now. Let me go—and I will ask the king to pardon all of you."

Robin pretended to believe him. "Do you swear it?"

"I do," vowed the sheriff.

"What of the silver we brought to serve you dinner?" Little John asked.

"What of the silver pennies and the bag of gold we found in the pitcher?" asked the cook.

"Keep it all," the sheriff said eagerly. "It is yours."

"Very well," Robin said. "But you must take back the horses that carried the silver. Silver and gold are pay enough for a night's bed and bread."

The outlaws brought the sheriff's horse and gave the huntsmen the reins of the other two. They cheered the sheriff as he galloped away.

"Well done," said Robin Hood to Little John. "We will sell the sheriff's table silver to add to his gold. With his gift we will feed the poor all winter long."

Only Will Stutely did not laugh. "We may have made a dangerous enemy," he said.

But Robin laughed. "We can worry about that tomorrow," he said. "Today is for making merry!"

And so they did.

THE SORROWFUL KNIGHT

The next day Little John went to Robin. "I see that there are rules to this robbing. Who besides the sheriff *may* we rob?"

"We do not rob women," Robin said. "Farmers and friars and all foot-travelers may pass by, too. So may friendly knights and squires. But bring abbots and archbishops to me. Tie them up and carry them if you must. Such churchmen are as greedy as the sheriff. They steal good farmers' lands to add to their own. They eat roast peacock and roast swan and honey cakes, and drink sweet wine. Yet poor men starve outside their doors."

"Fair enough," said Little John. "May God send us such a guest today!"

"We will not eat without one," Robin said. "Go, take your bow and Will Scarlet and Much. Walk north to the Roman road. The first stranger you meet there shall be our guest. Earl or baron or abbot or knight, bring him with you."

The wide Roman road was an hour's walk away. Little John and Will Scarlet and Much hurried. They hid in the bushes beside it to watch and wait. After a while they heard a faint *clip-clop, clip-clop*.

The rider was a sad-faced knight in a shabby cloak. His gray horse was as sorry-looking as he. The man's gray head hung low, and his horse's too. The man gave a sigh and the horse sighed, too.

Little John stepped to the center of the road.

"Greetings, Sir Knight," he said. "My master asks you to join him in the greenwood. Noonday dinner waits for you there."

"Who is your master?" the gloomy knight asked.

"Robin of Sherwood."

"Robin Hood? I hear he is a good man. Yes, I will come," the knight said. Yet he was as gloomy as before, or more. A tear rolled down his cheek as he rode along.

When they came to the outlaws' camp, Robin stepped forward. He pushed back his hood and knelt to greet the knight.

"I am Robin Hood. Welcome to Sherwood, Sir Knight."

The knight smiled a sad smile. "God save you, good Robin, and all your company. I am Sir Richard of Lee."

"Will you join us at our meat, Sir Richard?"

The knight nodded. "I will."

Robin and Sir Richard and the outlaws sat down

to their meal. They ate venison pie and pigeon pie and brown bread. They drank brown ale.

"Bless me," Sir Richard said. "I have not eaten this well in weeks."

"Good," Robin answered. "For you must pay before you go."

"Alas!" The knight shook his head. "I cannot pay. I have only ten shillings in my money box."

"So little?" said Robin. "If that is true, we will not take a penny. Have a look, Little John."

Little John went to the knight's horse. He untied the money box. He counted the shillings. There were only ten.

The knight wiped a tear away. "Two years ago I had all that I wanted and four hundred pounds more than I could spend. Now I have only my children and wife."

Robin was puzzled. "How can a knight be so poor?"

"My son entered a jousting contest," Sir Richard said. "Alas, by accident he killed the man he rode against. To pay the fine I sold all my goods. I borrowed on my lands. Tomorrow the loan falls due. If I do not repay four hundred pounds to the abbot of Saint Mary's Abbey, my lands are lost. I have only ten shillings, but still I must go."

He sighed and then stood. "So, thanks and farewell, good fellows."

"Do not be so hasty," Robin said. "We can lend what you need. But who will pledge to repay the loan if you cannot?"

"Alas!" The knight shook his head. "I have no friends left but God and Our Lady, Saint Mary."

"Agreed!" said Robin, to everyone's surprise. "No pledge could be safer than Our Lady's. Little John, go fetch four hundred pounds from our strongbox."

When Little John brought the four hundred pounds, he gave Robin a wink. "The good knight's suit is as shabby as he is sad," he whispered.

"You are right," agreed Robin. "Bring the box we took last month from the fat merchant of Mansfield."

The outlaws brought a trunk full of fine new clothes. From it Robin chose a tunic and cloak, and a hat and hose. Then his men brought bolts of cloth, scarlet and green and blue, for the knight to take home to his wife.

"Now he needs a horse to carry the cloth," Much said.

"A pair of boots," Will Scarlet added. "His own are worn and warped."

Little John nodded. "*And* a pair of gilt spurs."

The knight tried on his new clothes in a daze. Then, for the first time, he smiled. "God save you, Robin, and all of your men!"

The good knight mounted his horse. He took the reins of his new packhorse.

"Now name the day when I shall repay you," he said.

"A year from today," said Robin.

Sir Richard nodded. "A year from today. Under this greenwood tree."

SIR RICHARD AND THE ABBOT

The lord high justice and the sheriff of Nottingham came to Saint Mary's Abbey the next morning. Each had provided a share of the abbot's loan to Sir Richard of Lee.

The abbot wore a wide smile. "Today the knight of Lee must repay our four hundred pounds," he said. "I hope he cannot, for then his lands will be ours. They are worth ten times four hundred pounds."

The abbot was greedy, but most of the monks of Saint Mary's were good and godly men. The prior, the abbot's next-in-command, spoke up.

"It is still early. What if he is in trouble or in hardship on the road? It would be wrong of us to take his lands. Have you no conscience?"

"Pah!" the abbot snapped. "You are always in my beard. Where is Brother Cellarer? I have an errand for him."

"Here, my lord Abbot." The cellarer, a fat-faced

man, bowed low. His job was to keep the abbey supplied with food from its farms.

"Do not worry about the knight of Lee, my lord," the cellarer said. "I say the scoundrel is probably dead or hanged. His lands and all they grow and earn will be ours today."

The abbot smiled and sent the cellarer for a pitcher of the very best wine. Then he followed the sheriff and justice to the great hall. There they waited and ate and drank, ate and waited.

"He is not coming," the sheriff said at noon.

"He will not come," the justice said at two.

"He has not come!" the abbot crowed at four.

But at five o'clock Sir Richard came riding up the road. When he saw the abbey ahead, he smiled. Suddenly he turned aside into the trees. There he quickly changed back into his old, shabby clothes. Then he rode on.

The abbey gatekeeper opened the gate wide. "Welcome, Sir Knight. The lords wait for you. They are at their dinner. I will take your horses to the stable."

"No," the knight said. "Hold them here. I will not be long."

In the hall the abbot and justice and sheriff sat at a table heaped with food. There were silver pitchers of wine and silver plates. Silver platters held meats and fruits, honey cakes and sugar plums.

Sir Richard knelt. "I have come as I promised, Sir Abbot."

The abbot scowled. "Have you brought my money?"

"Alas, not a penny."

"I knew it!" The abbot laughed. Then he scowled again. "Why are you here, if you cannot pay?"

"To ask for more time," the knight said. "Good Sir

Justice, Sir Sheriff, Sir Abbot, be my friends. Hold my lands only until I can pay what I owe."

The abbot swore an angry oath. "It is too late, beggar knight! You get no lands from me."

"Nor from me," the justice said.

"Or me," said the sheriff.

"Your hearts are hard." Sir Richard rose to his feet. "And you are rude to keep an old man so long on his knees."

The knight took a money bag from under his cloak. He shook out four hundred pounds onto the table.

"There is your gold, Sir Abbot. If you had been kindhearted, I would have rewarded you with more."

The abbot gritted his teeth and glared.

Sir Richard stepped back and bowed.

"Sir Abbot and you men of law, farewell. Whether you like it or not, my lands are my own again."

In the courtyard, the knight changed back into his fine new clothes. The old ones he left where they fell. As he rode out through the abbey gate, he sang a merry song.

Hey down, derry, derry down,
A year from today in the greenwood!

ROBIN AND THE CELLARER

A year went by. Summer. Autumn. Winter. Spring. All year long Sir Richard of Lee farmed his lands. His workers sheared his sheep and cut his cabbages. They mowed his hay and cut his grain and picked his apples. They sold each crop at market.

At last the year was past, and Robin sat down under the greenwood tree to wait. Noonday came, but not Sir Richard.

Robin frowned. "I fear for our four hundred pounds. Perhaps Saint Mary will send it to us if the knight does not come."

"I say let us eat without him," grumbled Little John.

"I can wait," Robin said. "But if you are hungry, walk up to the Roman road. Bring us a stranger to share our meal."

Little John set off in a hurry with Will Scarlet and Much. When they reached the Roman road they hid in the bushes. Before long they saw two riders, far off.

The riders were monks in black robes, one fat and one thin. Behind them walked fifty-two men and seven packhorses.

Little John laughed to see them. "Oho!" he said. "I think these fellows have brought our pay. No bishop in the land rides out more royally."

"Make ready your bows," Will Scarlet warned.

"They are fifty-four and we are three," said Much. "But we must bring one of them with us. If we do not, we dare not face Robin."

"When I give the sign, shoot to miss," Little John whispered. He stepped into the middle of the road and aimed his bow.

"Stop where you are, rascal monk!" he called. "If you move, I will skewer you like a fat goose. Now, tell your men to run away home, or stay and be shot. Our master has a hundred bows in the bushes."

"Wh-Who is your master?" the fat monk asked.

"His name is Robin Hood," said proud Little John.

The monk turned pale. "Robin Hood the great thief? I have heard no good of him."

Little John gave a nod. At the signal, Will Scarlet and Much let fly arrow after arrow.

The thin monk wheeled his horse and galloped away. The men behind turned and ran as fast as their feet would carry them. No one stayed with the fat monk but a young page and the groom who led the packhorses.

Will stepped into the road. "Come, Sir Monk. Would you keep Robin waiting for his dinner?"

The three outlaws hurried the monk's horse along the forest road. The page and the groom with the packhorses trotted after them.

At the camp in the clearing Robin Hood came alone to greet them.

"Welcome, Sir Monk," he said. "Come, join us in our meal."

The monk folded his arms. His mouth was a tight, thin line. "I do not eat with robbers."

"Master," said Little John, "he has no manners."

Robin laughed. "Then we need to teach him some. Blow your horn."

The sound of the horn rang out. Men came running through the trees from all directions. Soon seventy and seven were gathered around Robin. Meekly the monk washed his hands and sat down at a long trestle table.

Robin Hood and Little John sat one on each side of him. They heaped his plate with good food.

"Eat well," Robin said. But the monk was too frightened to eat a bite.

"What abbey do you call home?" Robin asked.

"S-Saint Mary's Abbey. I am the cellarer there."

"Saint Mary's! Then you are twice welcome," Robin said. He gave the monk a goblet of wine. "I have been worried all day. I thought Our Lady had forgotten me. A knight promised in her name to repay money he borrowed from me. But I have not had my pay."

"Surely," Little John said, "this monk has brought it from her abbey."

"Have you, Sir Monk?" asked Robin. "Do you have my silver."

The unhappy monk looked from Little John to Robin and back again. He did not see Robin laugh behind his back.

"I swear," the cellarer said, "I know nothing of any payment from Saint Mary."

"You come from Our Lady's abbey. You *must* be her messenger," Robin said. "How much silver do you carry in your money box?"

"Only t-twenty marks."

"So little?" said Robin. "Then we will not take a penny. If we find more, it must be my payment from Saint Mary. We will not touch your twenty marks."

Little John went to find the packhorse that carried the money box. He spread his hood on the ground nearby. Then he opened the box and poured a shower of coins onto his hood. When he had counted them, he put twenty marks back and carried the rest to Robin.

"Eight hundred pounds more than twenty marks, Master."

"There! What did I tell you, Sir Monk?" Robin said. "And—wonder of wonders—Saint Mary has even

paid me double. Come, eat up and drink up!"

The monk grew as purple as a ripe plum. He would eat no meat and drink no wine. He rose from the table in anger.

The outlaws led him to his horse. They helped him mount. They tied his almost-empty money box on the packhorse's saddle. They waved and cheered as he rode off with his page and groom and the packhorses trotting behind. Robin stood with his hands on his hips and laughed.

"Thank your abbot for me," he called. "And your prior. Tell them to send me a monk like you to dinner every day!"

Sir Richard of Lee arrived at last. An hour before sunset he rode into Sherwood. A hundred archers marched behind him. The outlaws welcomed them all. They offered them cheese and apples and ale.

"Tell us," said Robin to the knight. "Did you pay off your loan? Did you save your lands?"

"Yes, thanks to God and to you," the knight said. "But I am almost late, and you have had to wait for your pay."

"No matter. You have kept your promise with an hour to spare."

"We started at dawn," Sir Richard said. "We traveled fast, but at noonday we came to Barnsley Bridge and a great wrestlers' fair. All the best wrestlers of the West Country were there."

Robin nodded. "And you stayed."

"And stayed and stayed," Sir Richard said sheepishly. "A stranger from the south won the last match. The prize was a horse and saddle and a red gold ring. The crowd wished to give them to their favorite instead."

"So you and your archers made sure the prize went to the stranger, who had earned it?" asked Robin.

"We did. Then I bought two barrels of ale for all to share," said Sir Richard.

"And stayed to help them drink it?" Robin Hood laughed.

Sir Richard laughed, too. He took a bag from his money box. "Here are the four hundred pounds you lent me, and twenty marks more for your kindness."

Robin waved the money away. "I cannot take it. Saint Mary sent her abbey's cellarer to repay the loan. I cannot collect it twice."

So Robin told the tale of the cellarer. The knight laughed loud and long when he heard it. Afterward he said, "And now I have a gift for you, my friends."

He beckoned to his men. They brought bundles and opened them for Robin and the outlaws to see. There were a hundred strong new longbows and a hundred sheaves of bright arrows.

"A fine gift indeed!" said Robin. "Little John, go to our strongbox. Bring the four hundred extra pounds the monk paid us. By right it should be Sir Richard's."

Little John brought the money.

"Take it," Robin said to the knight. "All the folk

who live on your lands depend upon you. Go home tomorrow, Sir Knight, and finish mending your fortunes. Then all of you may prosper together."

The next day Sir Richard set out to do just that.

Robin Hood and his men hunted the king's deer. They sheltered the homeless in Sherwood. They robbed rich travelers of gold and goods and gave them to the poor. They wrestled and shot at targets, told tales and sang songs, and ate and slept.

And life stayed peaceful in Sherwood for many a day.

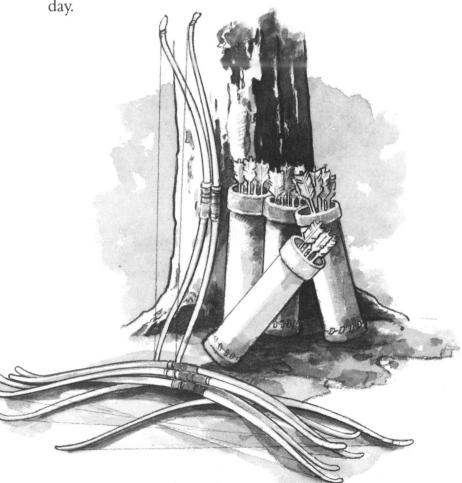

Some Words

An **abbey** is a place where a large group of **monks** live together like brothers. They have a church, a dormitory, a small hospital, gardens, and barns and farms.

An **abbot** is the churchman who is in charge of running an **abbey**.

An **archbishop** is a priest who is in charge of all the priests and churches in a wide area around the city in which his cathedral stands. (A **cathedral** is a very large and beautiful church.)

Earls and **barons** are English lords who were not as rich and powerful as princes or dukes, but were richer and more powerful than knights.

A **groom** is a man who works with horses. He "grooms" them so that they look their best, and feeds and saddles them.

Hose are full-length stockings with strings at the top to tie around the waist.

MONEY: The word **silver** is used to mean "money" as well as the metal itself. In England, **pound** is the name of the most important unit of money. In Robin Hood's time a **pound** was worth more than twenty present-day U.S. dollars. There were twenty **shill-**

ings in a **pound**. A **mark** was a coin worth thirteen shillings and four pence (four pennies).

A **monk** is a man who decides to live away from the bustle and violence of the world and closer to God. He lives with other monks in a monastery or **abbey**. He spends his time in work and prayer.

A **page** is a boy who serves a king or queen, lord or lady, or knight, or other important person. Often his parents were important people themselves, and the page was being trained in manners and taught about the grown-up world. He might have a number of different jobs, from carrying messages to serving his master at the dinner table.

A **pheasant** is a wild bird, very good to eat.

The **Roman road** in the story is one of many such roads in England. They were long, straight roads built by the Romans over fifteen hundred years ago.

A **squire** is a young man who serves a knight, and hopes to become one. In wartime he carried the knight's shield when the knight was not using it, and took care of the knight's armor. At other times he might have many duties, from holding his master's horse to providing dinner on their travels.

A **yeoman** is a farmer who owns and works his own land, or the son of such a farmer.